Treasury of

Mother Goose Rhymes

Cover illustration by
WENDY EDELSON

Border illustration by
JANE CHAMBLESS WRIGHT

Illustrations by
LISA BERRETT
KRISTA BRAUCKMANN-TOWNS
DREW-BROOK-CORMACK ASSOCIATES
WENDY EDELSON
JON GOODELL
KATE STURMAN GORMAN
JUDITH DUFOUR LOVE
BEN MAHAN
ANASTASIA MITCHELL
ANITA NELSON
LORI NELSON FIELD
DEBBIE PINKNEY
KAREN PRITCHETT
ROSARIO VALDERRAMA

PUBLICATIONS INTERNATIONAL, LTD.

Contents

Old MacDonald's Farm

The Hobbyhorse

I had a little hobbyhorse,
　　And it was dapple gray;
Its head was made of pea-straw,
　　Its tail was made of hay.

I sold it to an old woman
　　For a copper penny;
And I'll gladly sing my song again
　　If your horse should whinny!

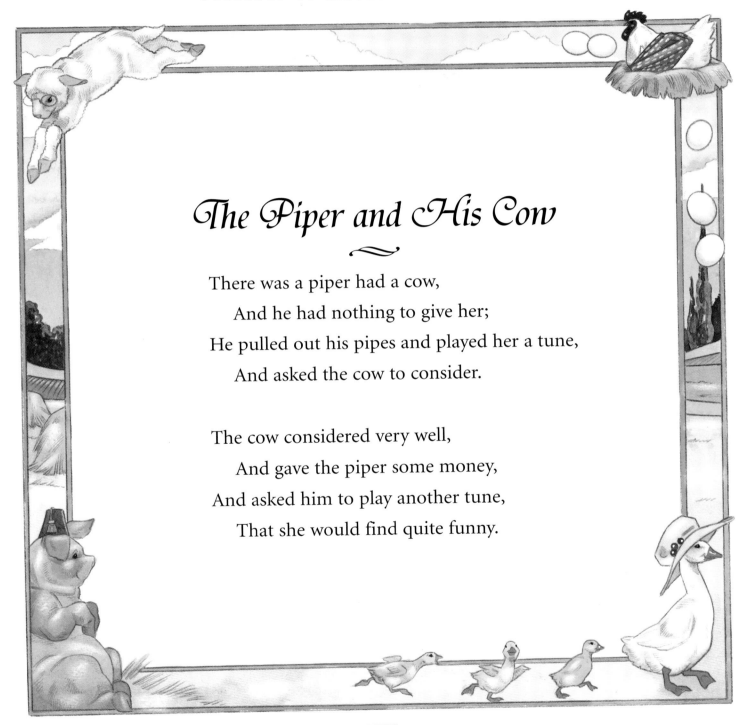

The Piper and His Cow

There was a piper had a cow,
And he had nothing to give her;
He pulled out his pipes and played her a tune,
And asked the cow to consider.

The cow considered very well,
And gave the piper some money,
And asked him to play another tune,
That she would find quite funny.

Shave a Pig

Barber, barber, shave a pig,
How many hairs will make a wig?
Four-and-twenty, that's enough.
Give the barber a pinch of snuff.

There Was a Little Pig

There was a little pig,
  Who wasn't very big,
So they put him in a great big show.
  While playing in the band,
He broke his little hand,
  And now he can't play his old banjo.

The Donkey

Donkey, donkey, old and gray,
　　Open your mouth and gently bray;
Lift your ears and blow your horn,
　　To wake the world this sleepy morn.

Bell Horses

Bell horses, bell horses,
What time of day?
One o'clock, two o'clock,
Three and away.

Robert Barnes

Robert Barnes, fellow fine,
Can you shoe this horse of mine?
Yes, good sir, that I can,
As well as any other man.
There's a nail, and there's a prod,
And now, good sir, your horse is shod.

A Horse and a Flea

A horse and a flea and three blind mice

Met each other while skating on ice.

The horse he slipped and fell on the flea.

The flea said, "Oops, there's a horse on me!"

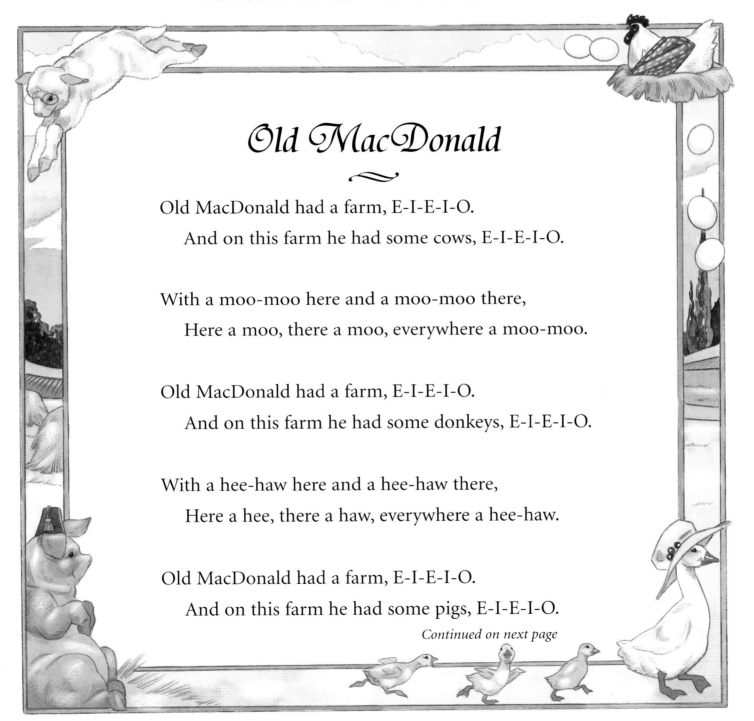

Old MacDonald

Old MacDonald had a farm, E-I-E-I-O.
　　And on this farm he had some cows, E-I-E-I-O.

With a moo-moo here and a moo-moo there,
　　Here a moo, there a moo, everywhere a moo-moo.

Old MacDonald had a farm, E-I-E-I-O.
　　And on this farm he had some donkeys, E-I-E-I-O.

With a hee-haw here and a hee-haw there,
　　Here a hee, there a haw, everywhere a hee-haw.

Old MacDonald had a farm, E-I-E-I-O.
　　And on this farm he had some pigs, E-I-E-I-O.

Continued on next page

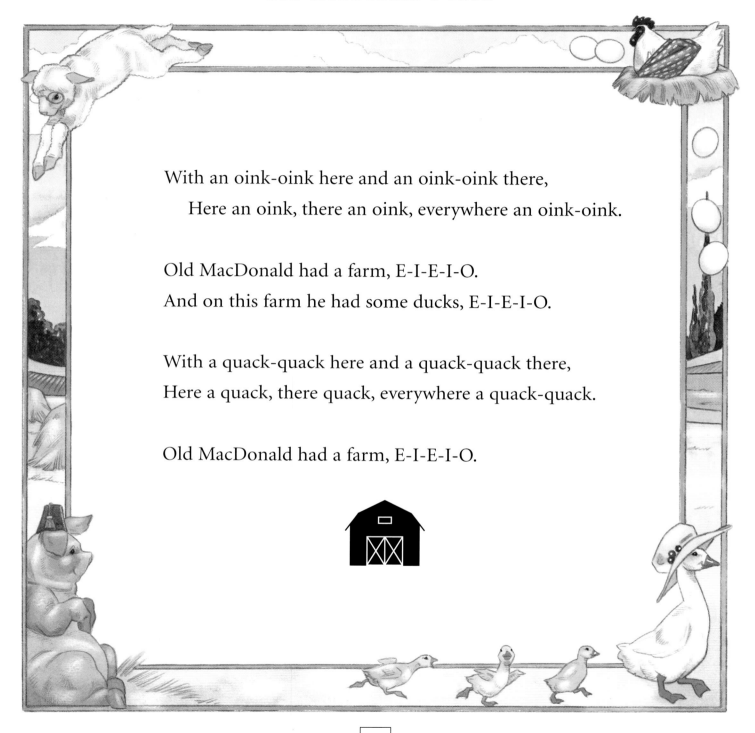

With an oink-oink here and an oink-oink there,
　　Here an oink, there an oink, everywhere an oink-oink.

Old MacDonald had a farm, E-I-E-I-O.
And on this farm he had some ducks, E-I-E-I-O.

With a quack-quack here and a quack-quack there,
Here a quack, there quack, everywhere a quack-quack.

Old MacDonald had a farm, E-I-E-I-O.

Dickery, Dickery, Dare

Dickery, dickery, dare,
　　The pig flew up in the air;
The man in brown soon brought him down,
　　Dickery, dickery, dare.

Charlie Warlie

Charlie Warlie had a cow,
  Black and white around the brow;
Open the gate and let her in,
  Charlie's cow is home again.

The Boy in the Barn

A little boy went into a barn,

And lay down on some hay.

An owl came out and flew about,

And the little boy ran away.

Upon My Word

Upon my word and honor
    As I went to Bonner,
I met a pig
    Without a wig,
Upon my word and honor.

The Little Mouse

I have seen you, little mouse,
Running all about the house,
Through the hole your little eye
In the wainscot peeping sly,
Hoping soon some crumbs to steal,
To make quite a hearty meal.
Look before you venture out,
See if kitty is about.

Mary Had a Little Lamb

Mary had a little lamb,

Its fleece was white as snow.

And everywhere that Mary went

The lamb was sure to go.

My Maid Mary

My maid Mary,
  She minds the dairy,
While I go a-hoeing
  And mowing each morn.
Gaily runs the reel
  And the spinning wheel,
While I am singing
  And mowing my corn.

Cushy Cow

Cushy cow, bonny, let down your milk,

And I will give you a gown of silk.

A gown of silk and a silver tee,

If you will let down your milk to me.

Cock-a-Doodle-Doo

Cock-a-doodle-doo,

   My dame has lost her shoe,

And master's lost his fiddling stick,

   Sing doodle-doodle-doo.

Baa, Baa, Black Sheep

Baa, baa, black sheep,
　　Have you any wool?
Yes, sir, yes, sir,
　　Three bags full:
One for the master,
　　One for the dame,
And one for the little boy
　　Who lives down the lane.

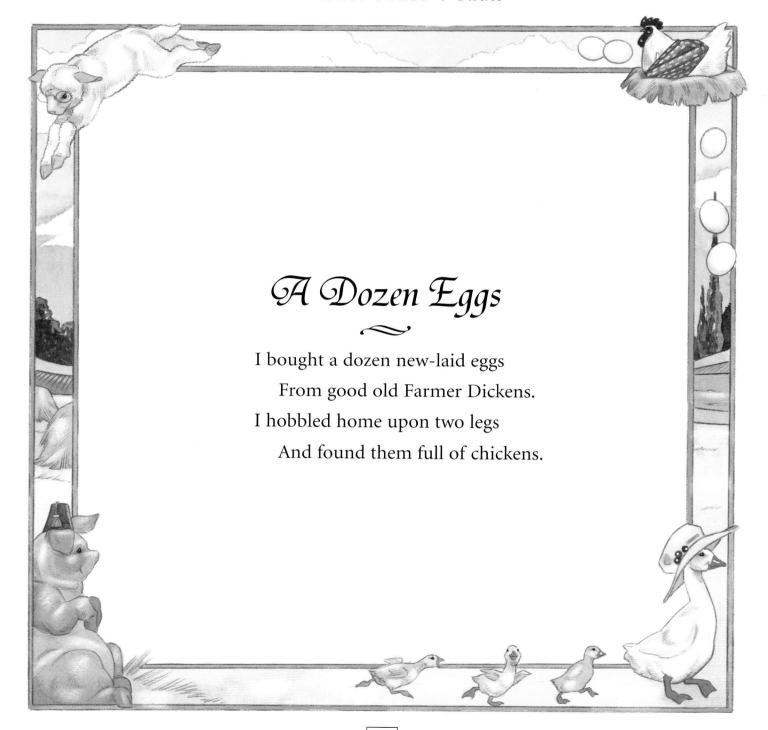

A Dozen Eggs

I bought a dozen new-laid eggs
    From good old Farmer Dickens.
I hobbled home upon two legs
    And found them full of chickens.

Three Blind Mice

Three blind mice, three blind mice;
 See how they run, see how they run!
They all ran after the farmer's wife,
 Who cut off their tails with a carving knife.
Have you ever seen such a sight
 In your life as three blind mice?

Young Lambs

If I'd as much money as I could tell,
I never would cry young lambs to sell.
Young lambs to sell, young lambs to sell,
I never would cry young lambs to sell.

The Learned Pig

My learned friend and neighbor pig,
   Odds bobs and bills, and dash my wig!
It's said that you the weather know.
   Please tell me when the wind will blow.

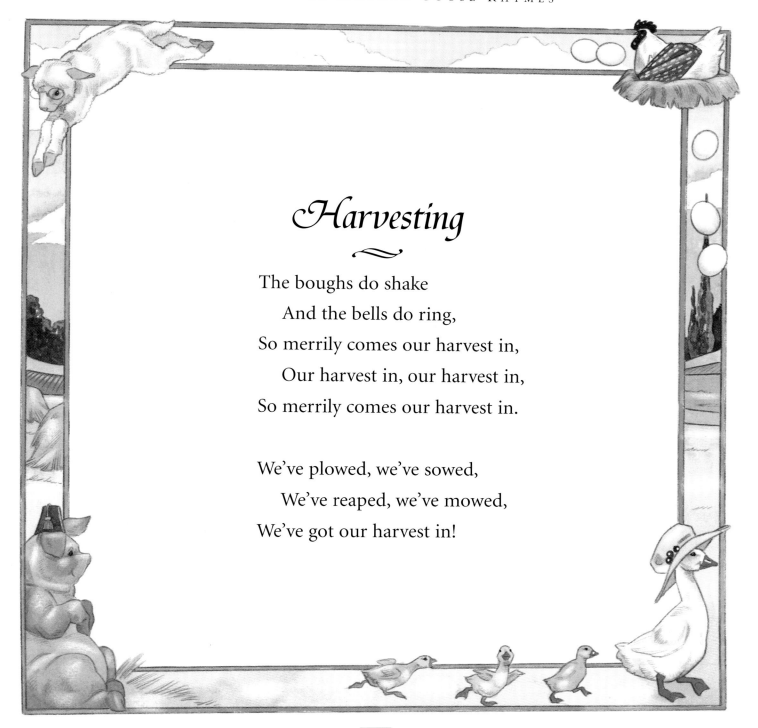

Harvesting

The boughs do shake
And the bells do ring,
So merrily comes our harvest in,
Our harvest in, our harvest in,
So merrily comes our harvest in.

We've plowed, we've sowed,
We've reaped, we've mowed,
We've got our harvest in!

The Purple Cow

I never saw a purple cow,

I hope I never see one;

But I can tell you, anyhow,

I'd rather see than be one.

Calendar Rhymes

Thirty Days Hath September

Thirty days hath September,
April, June, and November;
February has twenty-eight alone.
All the rest have thirty-one,
Excepting leap year, that's the time
When February has twenty-nine.

Play Days

How many days has my baby to play?

Saturday, Sunday, Monday,

Tuesday, Wednesday, Thursday, Friday;

Saturday, Sunday, Monday,

Hop away, skip away,

My baby wants to play.

My baby wants to play every day.

March Winds

～

March winds and April showers
Bring forth May flowers.

Calm in June

Calm weather in June
Sets corn in tune.

Saturday, Sunday

On Saturday night
Shall be all my care
To powder my locks
And curl my hair.

On Sunday morning
My love will come in,
When he will marry me
With a gold ring.

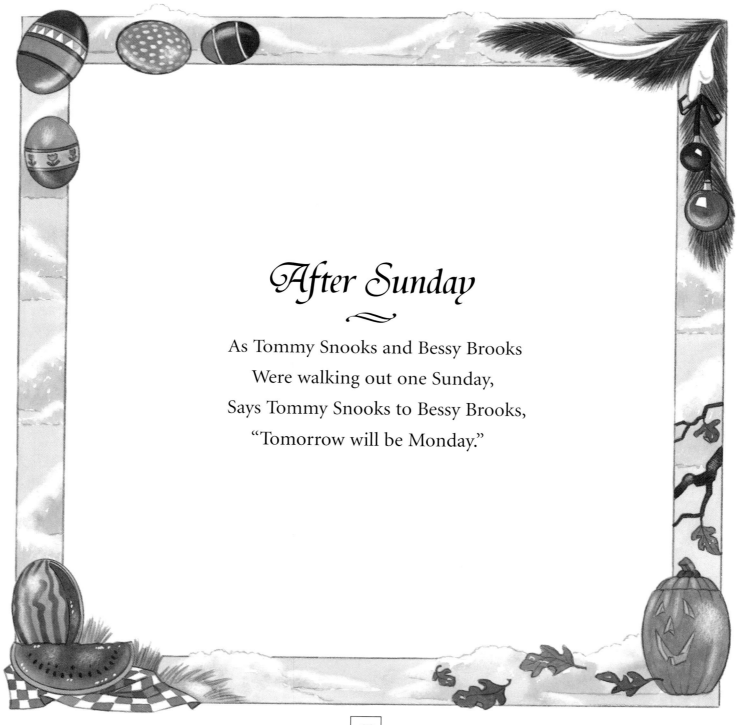

After Sunday

As Tommy Snooks and Bessy Brooks
Were walking out one Sunday,
Says Tommy Snooks to Bessy Brooks,
"Tomorrow will be Monday."

Winter

Cold and raw the north wind doth blow,

Bleak in the morning early.

All the hills are covered with snow,

And winter's now come fairly.

When the Snow Is on the Ground

The little robin grieves

When the snow is on the ground.

For the trees have no leaves,

And no berries can be found.

So toss around some crumbs of bread,

And then he'll eat 'til snow is gone.

A Week of Birthdays

Monday's child is fair of face,

Tuesday's child is full of grace,

Wednesday's child is full of woe,

Thursday's child has far to go,

Friday's child is loving and giving,

Saturday's child works hard for its living,

But the child that's born on the Sabbath day,

Is bonny and blithe, and good and gay.

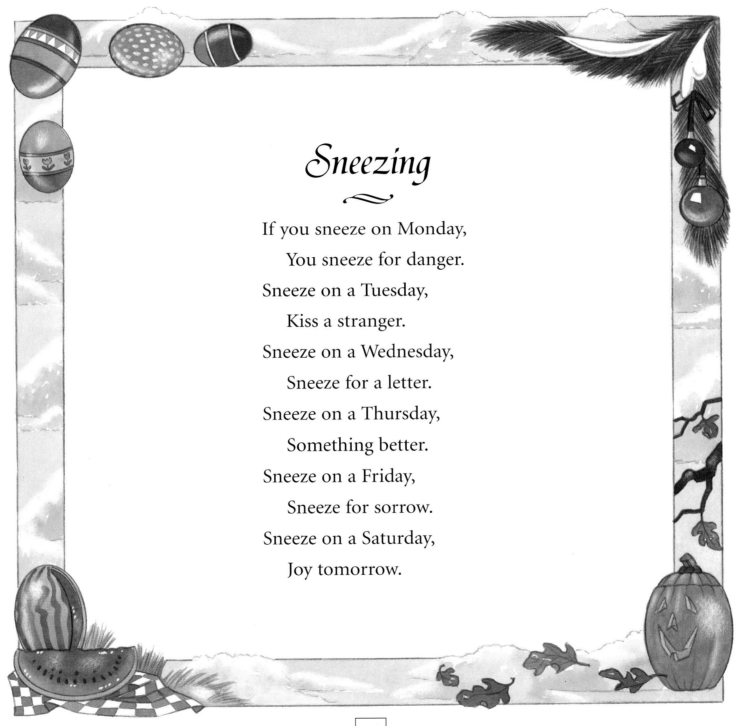

Sneezing

If you sneeze on Monday,
    You sneeze for danger.
Sneeze on a Tuesday,
    Kiss a stranger.
Sneeze on a Wednesday,
    Sneeze for a letter.
Sneeze on a Thursday,
    Something better.
Sneeze on a Friday,
    Sneeze for sorrow.
Sneeze on a Saturday,
    Joy tomorrow.

The Greedy Man

The greedy man is he who sits
  And bites bits out of plates,
Or else takes up a calendar
  And gobbles all the dates.

Silly
People
Rhymes

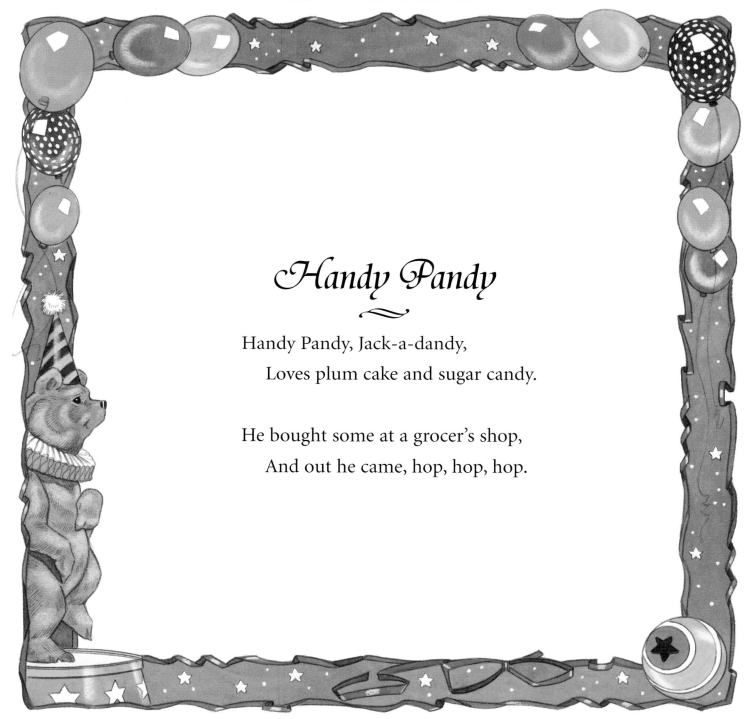

Handy Pandy

Handy Pandy, Jack-a-dandy,
    Loves plum cake and sugar candy.

He bought some at a grocer's shop,
    And out he came, hop, hop, hop.

The House That Jack Built

This is the house that Jack built.

This is the malt
    That lay in the house that Jack built.

This is the rat, that ate the malt,
    That lay in the house that Jack built.

This is the cat,
    That killed the rat, that ate the malt,
That lay in the house that Jack built.

This is the dog, that worried the cat,
    That killed the rat, that ate the malt,
That lay in the house that Jack built.

This is the cow with the crumpled horn,
That tossed the dog, that worried the cat,
That killed the rat, that ate the malt,
That lay in the house that Jack built.

This is the maiden all forlorn,
That milked the cow with the crumpled horn,
That tossed the dog, that worried the cat,
That killed the rat, that ate the malt,
That lay in the house that Jack built.

This is the man all tattered and torn,
That kissed the maiden all forlorn,
That milked the cow with the crumpled horn,
That tossed the dog, that worried the cat,
That killed the rat, that ate the malt,
That lay in the house that Jack built.

Continued on next page

This is the priest all shaven and shorn,
That married the man all tattered and torn,
That kissed the maiden all forlorn,
That milked the cow with the crumpled horn,
That tossed the dog, that worried the cat,
That killed the rat, that ate the malt,
That lay in the house that Jack built.

This is the farmer sowing his corn,
That kept the rooster that crowed in the morn,
That waked the priest all shaven and shorn,
That married the man all tattered and torn,
That kissed the maiden all forlorn,
That milked the cow with the crumpled horn,
That tossed the dog, that worried the cat,
That killed the rat, that ate the malt,
That lay in the house that Jack built.

Mary, Mary

Mary, Mary, quite contrary,
How does your garden grow?
With silver bells and cockleshells,
And pretty maids all in a row.

Peter White

Peter White will ne'er go right,
    And would you know the reason why?
He follows his nose wherever he goes,
    And all that stands awry.

The Piper's Son

Tom, Tom, the piper's son,
Stole a pig and away he run!
The pig thought it was quite a treat,
To be carried down the street.

Lucy Locket

Lucy Locket lost her pocket,

Kitty Fisher found it;

Not a penny was there in it,

Only ribbon round it.

Nothing-at-All

There was an old woman called Nothing-at-all,
Who lived in a dwelling exceedingly small;
A man stretched his mouth to the utmost extent,
And down in one gulp house and old woman went.

Miss Mackay

Alas, alas, for Miss Mackay!
Her knives and forks have run away.
And where the cups and spoons are going,
She's sure there is no way of knowing.

Anna Elise

Anna Elise,

    She jumped with surprise.

The surprise was so quick,

    It played her a trick.

The trick was so rare,

    She jumped in a chair.

The chair was so frail,

    She jumped in a pail.

The pail was so wet,

    She jumped in a net.

The net was so small,

    She jumped on a ball.

The ball was so round,

    She jumped on the ground.

And ever since then

    She's been turning around.

The Old Woman

The old woman stands at the tub, tub, tub,

The dirty clothes to rub, rub, rub;

But when they are clean and fit to be seen,

She'll dress like a lady and dance on the green.

Rub-a-Dub-Dub

Rub-a-dub-dub,

    Three men in a tub,

And how do you think they got there?

    The butcher, the baker,

The candlestick maker,

    They all jumped out of a rotten potato,

'Twas enough to make a man stare.

The Old Woman Under the Hill

There was an old woman

Lived under a hill;

And if she's not gone,

She lives there still.

Old Soldier of Bister

There was an old soldier of Bister,
  Went walking one day with his sister,
When a cow at a poke
  Tossed her into an oak
Before the old gentleman missed her.

If Wishes Were Horses

If wishes were horses,

Beggars would ride.

If turnips were watches,

I would wear one by my side.

And if "ifs" and "ands"

Were pots and pans,

There'd be no work for tinkers!

Lock and Key

"I am a gold lock."

"I am a gold key."

"I am a silver lock."

"I am a silver key."

"I am a brass lock."

"I am a brass key."

"I am a lead lock."

"I am a lead key."

"I am a don lock."

"I am a don key!"

Three Wise Men

Three wise men of Gotham
Went to sea in a bowl.
If the bowl had been stronger,
My song would be longer.

Solomon Grundy

Solomon Grundy,
Born on Monday,
Christened on Tuesday,
Married on Wednesday,
Took ill on Thursday,
Worse on Friday,
Died on Saturday,
Buried on Sunday.
This is the end of Solomon Grundy.

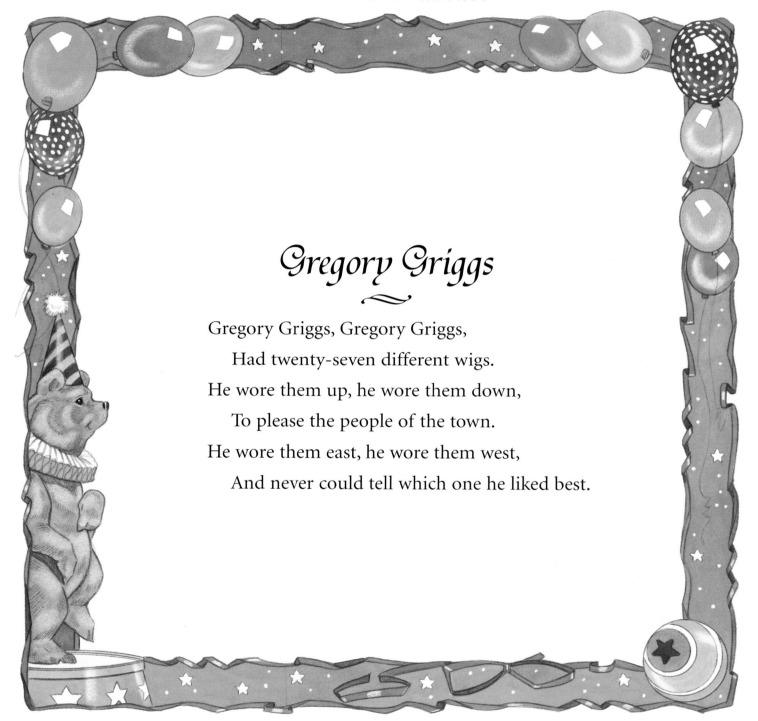

Gregory Griggs

Gregory Griggs, Gregory Griggs,
Had twenty-seven different wigs.
He wore them up, he wore them down,
To please the people of the town.
He wore them east, he wore them west,
And never could tell which one he liked best.

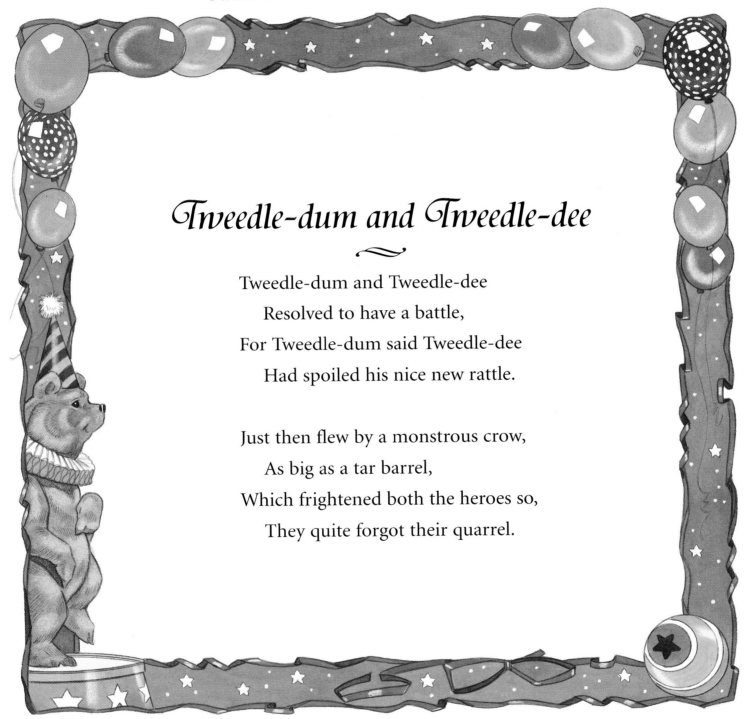

Tweedle-dum and Tweedle-dee

Tweedle-dum and Tweedle-dee
Resolved to have a battle,
For Tweedle-dum said Tweedle-dee
Had spoiled his nice new rattle.

Just then flew by a monstrous crow,
As big as a tar barrel,
Which frightened both the heroes so,
They quite forgot their quarrel.

Moses' Toeses

Moses supposes his toeses are roses,

But Moses supposes erroneously.

For nobody's toeses are posies of roses

As Moses supposes his toeses to be.

Play-Along Rhymes

Here We Go Round the Mulberry Bush

Here we go round the mulberry bush,
The mulberry bush, the mulberry bush,
Here we go round the mulberry bush,
On a cold and frosty morning.

Pat-a-Cake

Pat-a-cake, pat-a-cake,
Baker's man!
Bake me a cake,
As fast as you can.
Pat it, and prick it,
And mark it with a B.
Put it in the oven
For Baby and me.

Rain, Rain, Go Away

Rain, rain, go away,
Come again another day;
Little Johnny wants to play.

A Sure Test

If you are to be a gentlemen,

As I suppose you'll be,

You'll neither laugh nor smile,

For a tickling of the knee.

Here Sits the Lord Mayor

Here sits the Lord Mayor.

Here sit his two men.

Here sit the ladies.

Here sits the hen.

Here sit the little chickens.

Here they run in.

Billy, Billy

Billy, Billy, come and play,
    While the sun shines bright as day.
Yes, my Polly, so I will,
    For I love to please you still.
Billy, Billy, have you seen
    Sam and Betsy on the green?
Yes, my dear I saw them pass,
    Skipping over the new-mown grass.
Billy, Billy, come along,
    And I will sing a pretty song.

Georgie Porgie

Georgie Porgie, pudding and pie,

    Kissed the girls and made them cry.

When the boys came out to play,

    Georgie Porgie ran away.

Come Out to Play

Girls and boys,
     Come out to play.
The moon doth shine
     As bright as day.
Leave your supper,
     And leave your sleep,
And come play with your playfellows
     Into the street.

Little Jumping Joan

Here I am,
    Little Jumping Joan.
When nobody's with me,
    I'm all alone.

This Little Piggy

This little piggy went to market.
This little piggy stayed home.
This little piggy had roast beef.
This little piggy had none.
This little piggy cried,
"Wee-wee-wee,"
All the way home.

Swim

Mother, may I go out to swim?
Yes, my darling daughter.
Hang your clothes on a hickory limb
And don't go near the water.

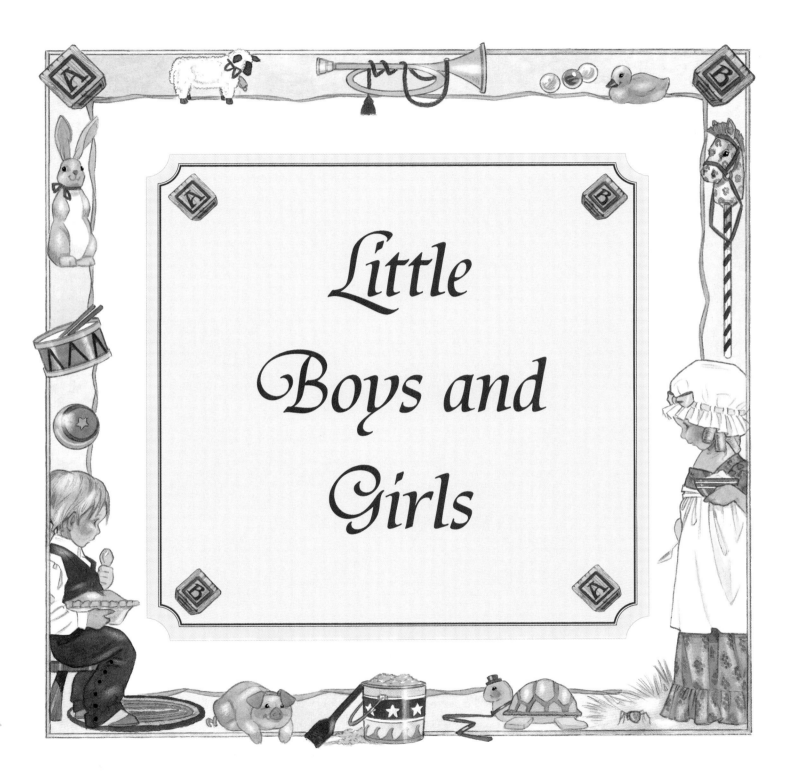

Little Boys and Girls

Little Jack Horner

Little Jack Horner
    Sat in a corner
Eating his Christmas pie;

He put in his thumb,
    And pulled out a plum,
And cried, "What a good boy am I!"

Blue Bell Boy

I had a little boy,
     And called him Blue Bell;
Gave him a little work,
     He did it very well.

I made him go upstairs
     To bring me a gold pin;
In a coal bucket fell he,
     Up to his little chin.

He went to the cellar
     To draw a little chair;
And quickly did return
     To say there was none there.

There Was a Little Girl

There was a little girl, who had a little curl,
    Right in the middle of her forehead,
And when she was good, she was very, very good.
    But when she was bad, she was horrid.

She stood on her head, on her little trundle bed,
    With no one there to say "no,"
She screamed and she squalled, she yelled and she bawled,
    And drummed her little heels against the window.

Her mother heard the noise, and thought it was the toys,
    Falling in the dusty attic,
She rushed up the flight, and saw she was alright,
    And hugged her most emphatic.

Freddie and the Cherry Tree

Freddie saw some fine ripe cherries
    Hanging on a cherry tree.
And he said, "You pretty cherries,
    Will you not come down to me?"

"Thank you kindly," said a cherry,
    "We would rather stay up here;
If we ventured down this morning,
    You would eat us up, I fear."

One, the finest of the cherries,
    Dangled from a slender twig.
"You are beautiful," said Freddie,
    "Red and ripe, and oh, how big!"

Continued on next page

"Catch me," said the cherry, "catch me,
Little master, if you can."
"I would catch you very soon," said Freddie,
"If I were a grown-up man."

Freddie jumped, and tried to reach it,
Standing high upon his toes;
But the cherry bobbed about,
And laughed, and tickled Freddie's nose.

"Never mind," said little Freddie,
"I shall have them when it's right."
But a blackbird whistled boldly,
"I shall have them all tonight."

Little Fred

When Little Fred went to bed,

He always said his prayers;

He kissed his mama, and then papa,

And straightaway went upstairs.

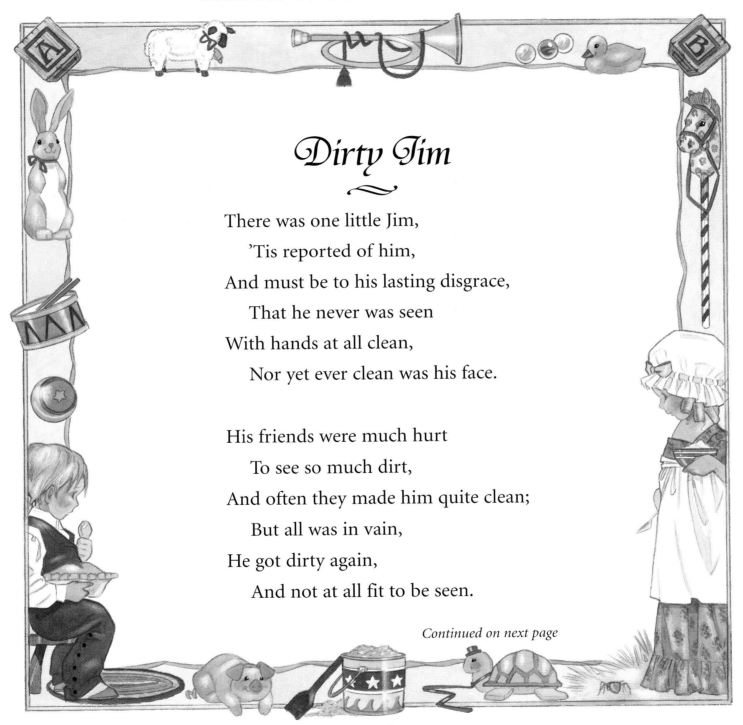

Dirty Jim

There was one little Jim,
'Tis reported of him,
And must be to his lasting disgrace,
That he never was seen
With hands at all clean,
Nor yet ever clean was his face.

His friends were much hurt
To see so much dirt,
And often they made him quite clean;
But all was in vain,
He got dirty again,
And not at all fit to be seen.

Continued on next page

135

It gave him no pain
  To hear them complain,
Nor his own dirty clothes to survey;
  His indolent mind
No pleasure could find
  In tidy and wholesome array.

Though unkempt and messy,
  Unlike his friend Jessie,
Jim loved dirty ways to be sure;
  But neat kids are seen,
To be decent and clean,
  And their smiles are ever so pure.

My Little Maid

High diddle doubt, my candle's out
My little maid is not at home;
Saddle my hog and bridle my dog,
And fetch my little maid home.

Little Miss Muffet

Little Miss Muffet
   Sat on a tuffet,
Eating her curds and whey.
   There came a big spider,
Who sat down beside her
   And frightened Miss Muffet away.

My Little Brother

Little brother, darling boy
    You are very dear to me!
I am happy—full of joy,
    When your smiling face I see.

How I wish that you could speak,
    And could know the words I say!
Pretty stories I would seek—
    To amuse you every day.

Shake your rattle—here it is—
    Listen to its merry noise;
And, when you are tired of this,
    I will bring you other toys.

My Little Sister

I have a little sister,
　　She is only two years old;
But to us at home who love her,
　　She is worth her weight in gold.

We often play together;
　　And I begin to find,
That to make my sister happy,
　　I must be very kind;

I must not taunt or tease her,
　　Or ever angry be
With the darling little sister
　　That God has given to me.

Jack Jelf

Little Jack Jelf
    Was put upon a shelf
Because he could not spell "pie;"
    When his aunt, Mrs. Grace,
Saw his sorrowful face,
    She could not help saying, "Oh, my!"

And since Master Jelf
    Was put upon the shelf
Because he could not spell "pie,"
    Let him stand there so grim,
And no more about him,
    For I wish him a very good-bye!

Little Polly Flinders

Little Polly Flinders
　　Sat among the cinders
Warming her pretty little toes;
　　Her mother came and stopped her,
For fear her lovely daughter
　　Would toast her pretty little nose.

Patience Is a Virtue

Patience is a virtue,

Virtue is a grace,

Grace is a little girl

Who wouldn't wash her face.

Busy-time Rhymes

Old Woman, Old Woman

There was an old woman
    Tossed up in a basket,
Nineteen times as high as the moon.
    Where was she going?
I couldn't but ask it,
    For in her hand she carried a broom.

Old woman, old woman,
    Old woman, said I,
O whither, O whither,
    O whither, so high?
To brush the cobwebs off the sky!
    And I'll be back again by and by.

Willy Boy

Willy boy, Willy boy,
  Where are you going?
I will go with you,
  If that I may.

I'm going to the meadow
  To see them a-mowing;
I'm going to help them
  To make the hay.

To Market

To market, to market, to buy a fat pig,

Home again, home again, jiggety-jig.

To market, to market, to buy a fat hog,

Home again, home again, jiggety-jog.

Jack

All work and no play makes

Jack a dull boy.

All play and no work makes

Jack a mere toy.

The Old Woman of Leeds

There was an old woman of Leeds,

Who spent her time in good deeds.

She worked for the poor

Till her fingers were sore,

This pious old woman of Leeds!

Old Chairs

If I'd as much money as I could spend,
 I never would cry old chairs to mend.
Old chairs to mend, old chairs to mend,
 I never would cry old chairs to mend.
If I'd as much money as I could tell,
 I never would cry old clothes to sell.
Old clothes to sell, old clothes to sell,
 I never would cry old clothes to sell.

Peter Piper

Peter Piper picked a peck
  Of pickled peppers;
A peck of pickled peppers
  Peter Piper picked.

If Peter Piper picked a peck
  Of pickled peppers,
Where's the peck of pickled peppers
  Peter Piper picked?

Sweep

Sweep, sweep, chimney sweep,
From the bottom to the top.
Sweep it all up, chimney sweep,
From the bottom to the top.

Shopping Robins

A robin and a robin's son
    Once went to town to buy a bun.
They could not decide
    On plum or plain,
And so they went back home again.

I Love You Rhymes

Lavender Blue

Lavender blue and rosemary green,
When I am king you shall be queen;
Call up my maids at four o'clock,
Some to the wheel and some to the rock;
Some to make hay and some to shear corn,
And you and I will sing until morn.

A Fish for You

There once was a fish.

   (What more could you wish?)

He lived in the sea.

   (Where else would he be?)

He was caught on a line.

   (Whose line if not mine?)

So I brought him to you.

   (What else should I do?)

Hoddley, Poddley

Hoddley, poddley,
  Puddles and fogs,
Cats are to marry
  Poodle dogs.
Cats in blue jackets
  And dogs in red hats,
What will become of
  The mice and the rats?

The Deer

The deer he loves the high wood,
The hare she loves the hill;
The knight he loves his bright sword,
The lady—loves her will.

Burnie Bee

Burnie Bee, Burnie Bee,
Tell me when your wedding will be.
If it be tomorrow day,
Take your wings and fly away.

Why May I Not Love Jenny

Jenny shall have a new bonnet,
And Jenny shall go to the fair,
And Jenny shall have a blue ribbon
To tie up her bonny brown hair.

And why may I not love Jenny?
And why may not Jenny love me?
And why may I not love Jenny
As well as another body?

My Love

Have you seen my love
    Coming from the market?
A peck of meal upon her back,
    A baby in her basket;
Have you seen my love
    Coming from the market?

Fiddle-De-Dee

Fiddle-de-dee, Fiddle-de-dee,

The fly shall marry the bumblebee.

They went to church, and married was she;

The fly had married the bumblebee.

I Love Coffee

I love coffee,

I love tea,

I love the girls,

and they love me.

Boy and Girl

There was a little boy and a little girl
    Lived in an alley;
Says the little boy to the little girl,
    "Shall I, oh, shall I?"
Says the little girl to the little boy,
    "What shall we do?"
Says the little boy to the little girl,
    "I will kiss you."

He Loves Me

He loves me. He don't!

He'll have me. He won't!

He would if he could.

But he can't. So he don't.

Curly Locks

Curly locks, Curly locks, will you be mine?

You will not wash dishes nor yet feed the swine,

But sit on a cushion and sew a fine seam,

And feed upon strawberries, sugar, and cream.

I Shall Be Married

Oh, Mother, I shall be married to
    Mr. Punchinello,
To Mr. Punch,
    To Mr. Joe,
To Mr. Nell,
    To Mr. Lo,
To Mr. Punch, Mr. Joe, Mr. Nell, Mr. Lo,
    To Mr. Punchinello.

Molly, My Sister

Molly, my sister, and I fell out,

    And what do you think it was all about?

She loved coffee and I loved tea,

    And that was the reason we couldn't agree.

Riddle Rhymes

Going to St. Ives

As I was going to St. Ives,

I met a man with seven wives.

Every wife had seven sacks.

Every sack had seven cats.

Every cat had seven kits.

Kits, cats, sacks, and wives,

How many were going to St. Ives?

One.

Daffy's Dress

Daffy-down-dilly has come to town

In a yellow petticoat and a green gown.

What is it?

A daffodil.

Nanny Etticoat

Little Nanny Etticoat
With a white petticoat,
And a red nose;
The longer she stands,
The shorter she grows.

What is she?
A candle.

Elizabeth

Elizabeth, Lizzy, Betsy, and Bess,
　　They all went together to seek a bird's nest.
They found a bird's nest with five eggs in,
　　If they all took one out,

How many were in?
Four.

See Me

Read my riddle, I pray.

What God never sees,

What the king seldom sees,

What we see every day.

What is it?
An equal.

Winter Blossom

Lives in winter,

  Dies in summer,

And grows with its roots upward!

What is it?

An icicle.

Riddle Me This

Riddle me, riddle me, what is that?
Over the head and under the hat?

What is this?
Hair.

No Nose

~

A riddle, a riddle, as I suppose,

    A hundred eyes and never a nose!

What is it?

A potato.

Four Corners

Black within and red without;
Four corners round about.

What is it?

A Chimney.

Fashion Seasons

In spring I look gay,
    Decked in comely array.
In summer more clothing I wear.

When colder it grows,
    I fling off my clothes,
And in winter quite naked appear.

What is it?
A tree.

A Recipe Riddle

Flour of England, fruit of Spain,

Met together in a shower of rain.

Put in a bag tied round with a string.

If you'll tell me this riddle,

I'll give you a ring.

What is it?
Plum pudding.

White Horses

Thirty white horses upon a red hill,
   Now they tramp, now they champ,
Now they stand still.

What are they?
Teeth.

Feathered Friends

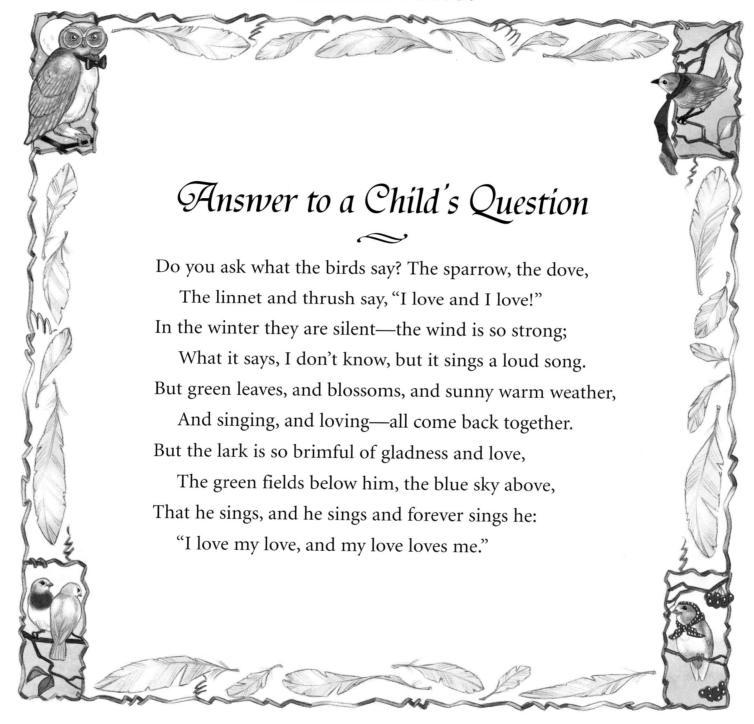

Answer to a Child's Question

Do you ask what the birds say? The sparrow, the dove,
    The linnet and thrush say, "I love and I love!"
In the winter they are silent—the wind is so strong;
    What it says, I don't know, but it sings a loud song.
But green leaves, and blossoms, and sunny warm weather,
    And singing, and loving—all come back together.
But the lark is so brimful of gladness and love,
    The green fields below him, the blue sky above,
That he sings, and he sings and forever sings he:
    "I love my love, and my love loves me."

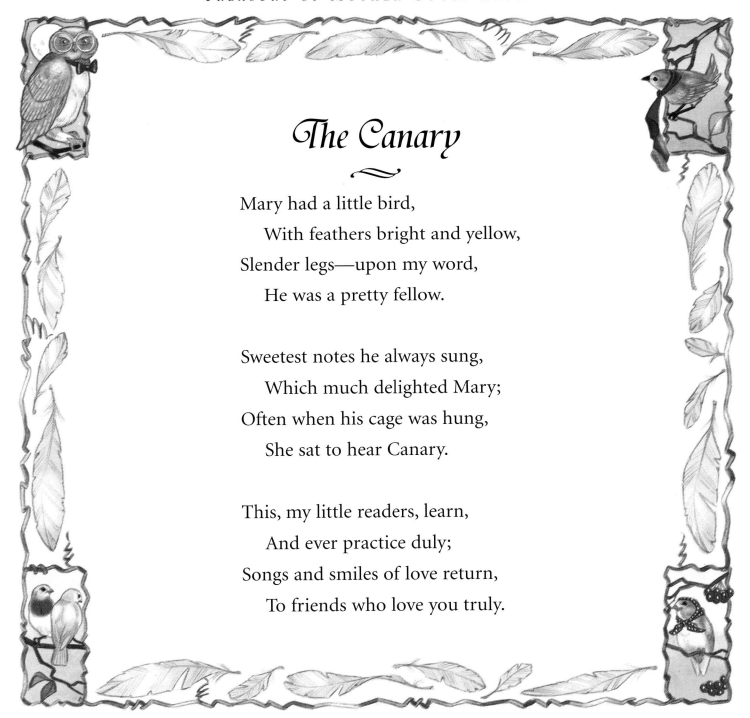

The Canary

Mary had a little bird,
    With feathers bright and yellow,
Slender legs—upon my word,
    He was a pretty fellow.

Sweetest notes he always sung,
    Which much delighted Mary;
Often when his cage was hung,
    She sat to hear Canary.

This, my little readers, learn,
    And ever practice duly;
Songs and smiles of love return,
    To friends who love you truly.

The Duck

Behold the duck.

 It does not cluck.

A cluck it lacks.

 It quacks.

'Tis especially fond

 Of a puddle or pond.

When it dines or sups,

 It bottoms up.

The Robin

When up aloft
    I fly and fly
I see in pools
    The shining sky,
And a happy bird
    Am I, am I!

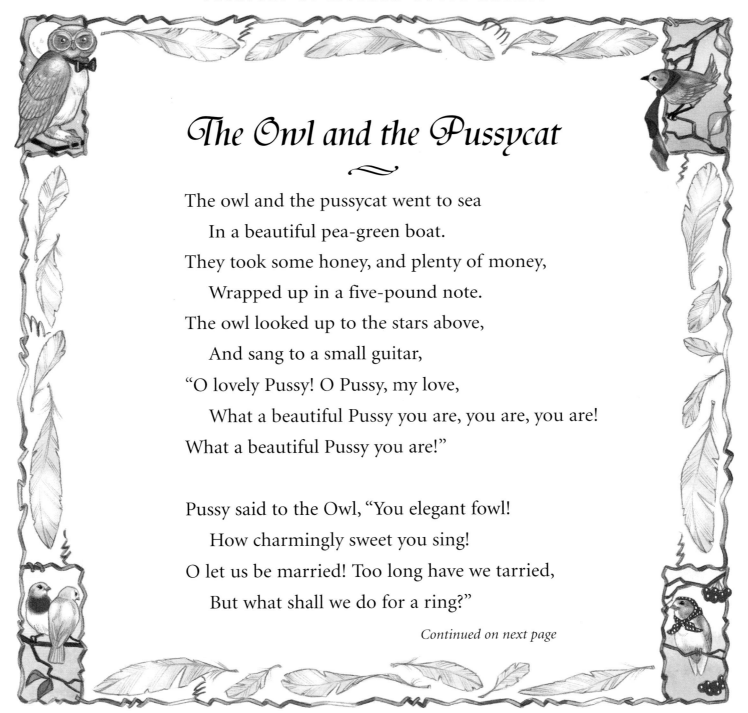

The Owl and the Pussycat

The owl and the pussycat went to sea
    In a beautiful pea-green boat.
They took some honey, and plenty of money,
    Wrapped up in a five-pound note.
The owl looked up to the stars above,
    And sang to a small guitar,
"O lovely Pussy! O Pussy, my love,
    What a beautiful Pussy you are, you are, you are!
What a beautiful Pussy you are!"

Pussy said to the Owl, "You elegant fowl!
    How charmingly sweet you sing!
O let us be married! Too long have we tarried,
    But what shall we do for a ring?"

Continued on next page

213

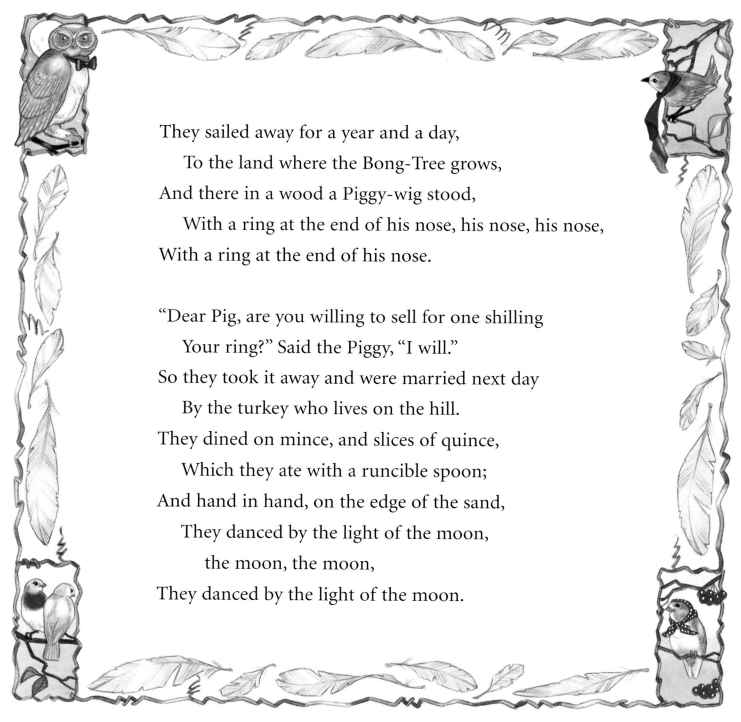

They sailed away for a year and a day,
    To the land where the Bong-Tree grows,
And there in a wood a Piggy-wig stood,
    With a ring at the end of his nose, his nose, his nose,
With a ring at the end of his nose.

"Dear Pig, are you willing to sell for one shilling
    Your ring?" Said the Piggy, "I will."
So they took it away and were married next day
    By the turkey who lives on the hill.
They dined on mince, and slices of quince,
    Which they ate with a runcible spoon;
And hand in hand, on the edge of the sand,
    They danced by the light of the moon,
        the moon, the moon,
They danced by the light of the moon.

Time to Rise

A birdie with a yellow bill

    Hopped upon the window sill,

Tipped his shining eye, and said:

    "Aren't you ashamed, you sleepy-head?"

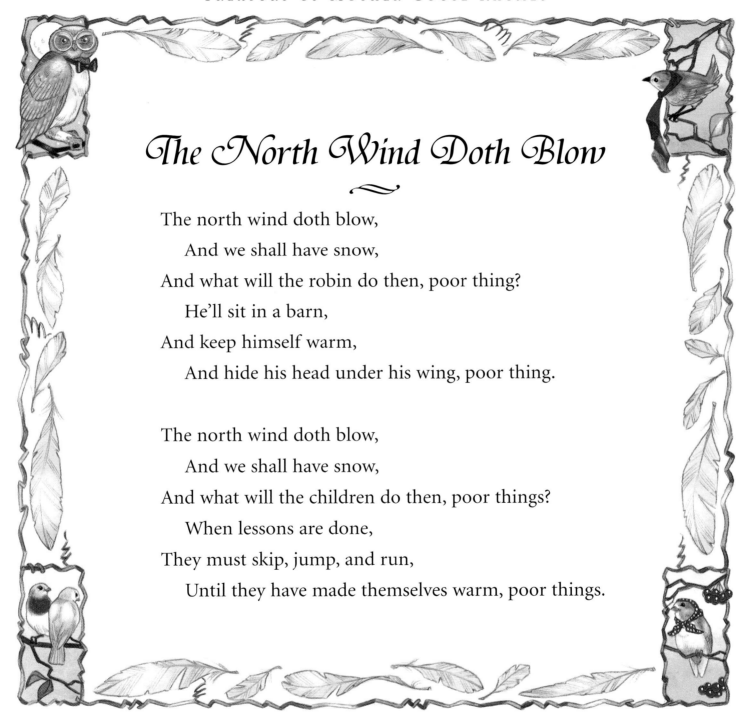

The North Wind Doth Blow

The north wind doth blow,
  And we shall have snow,
And what will the robin do then, poor thing?
  He'll sit in a barn,
And keep himself warm,
  And hide his head under his wing, poor thing.

The north wind doth blow,
  And we shall have snow,
And what will the children do then, poor things?
  When lessons are done,
They must skip, jump, and run,
  Until they have made themselves warm, poor things.

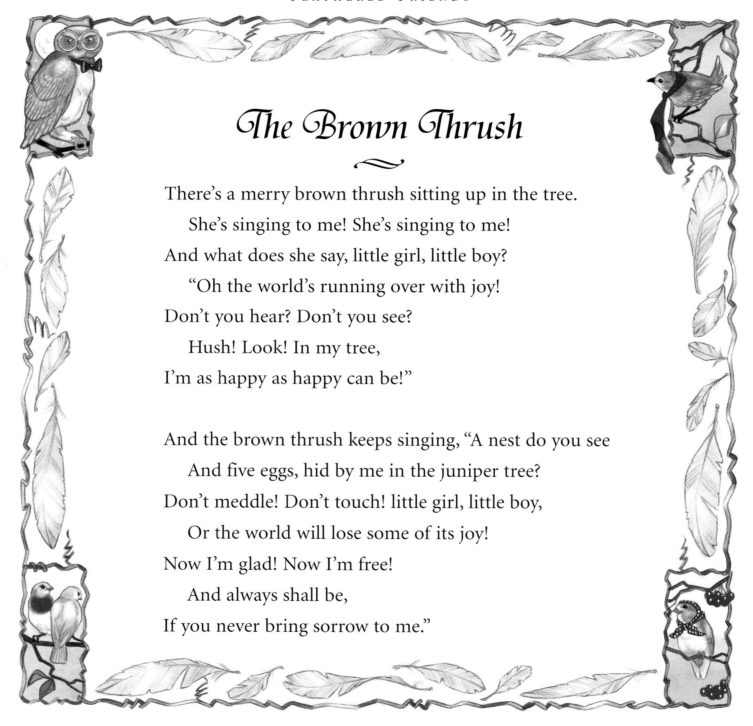

The Brown Thrush

There's a merry brown thrush sitting up in the tree.
    She's singing to me! She's singing to me!
And what does she say, little girl, little boy?
    "Oh the world's running over with joy!
Don't you hear? Don't you see?
    Hush! Look! In my tree,
I'm as happy as happy can be!"

And the brown thrush keeps singing, "A nest do you see
    And five eggs, hid by me in the juniper tree?
Don't meddle! Don't touch! little girl, little boy,
    Or the world will lose some of its joy!
Now I'm glad! Now I'm free!
    And always shall be,
If you never bring sorrow to me."

So the merry brown thrush sings away in the tree,
 To you and to me, to you and to me;
And she sings all the day, little girl, little boy,
 "Oh the world's running over with joy!
But long it won't be
 Don't you know? Don't you see?
Unless we're as good as can be."

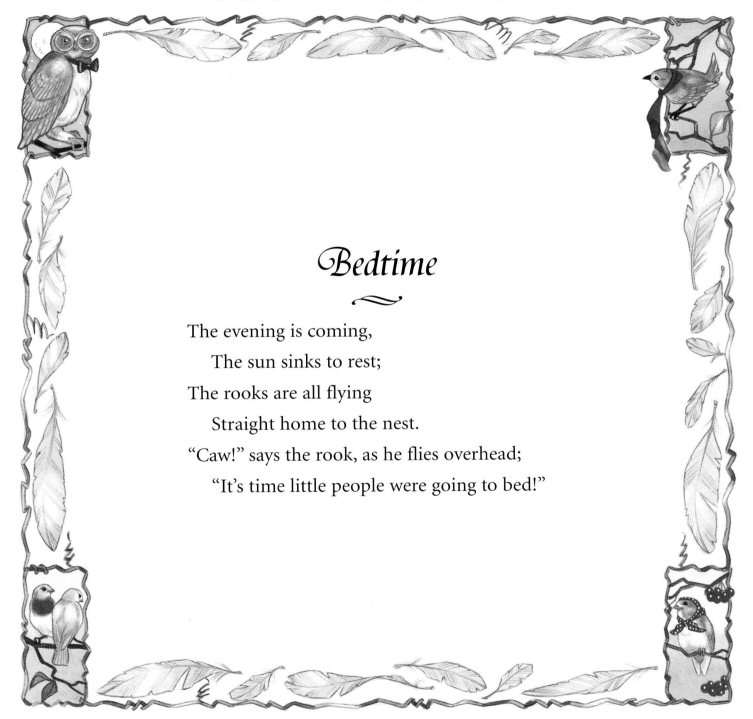

Bedtime

The evening is coming,
  The sun sinks to rest;
The rooks are all flying
  Straight home to the nest.
"Caw!" says the rook, as he flies overhead;
  "It's time little people were going to bed!"

The Owl

When cats run home and light is come,
And dew is cold upon the ground,
And the far-off stream is dumb,
And the whirring sail goes round,
And the whirring sail goes round;
Alone and warming his five wits,
The white owl in the belfry sits.

When merry milkmaids click the latch,
And sweetly smells the new-mown hay,
And the rooster sings beneath the thatch,
Twice or thrice his roundelay,
Twice or thrice his roundelay;
Alone and warming his five wits,
The white owl in the belfry sits.

Robin Redbreast

Little Robin Redbreast
　　Sat upon a tree.
Up went Pussycat;
　　Down went he.
Down came Pussycat;
　　Away Robin ran.
Says little Robin Redbreast,
　　"Catch me if you can!"

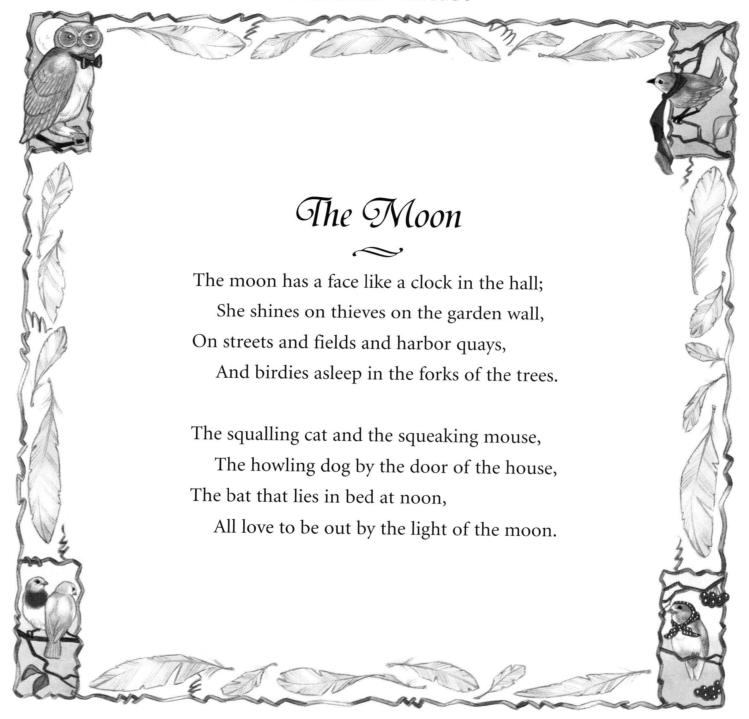

The Moon

The moon has a face like a clock in the hall;
    She shines on thieves on the garden wall,
On streets and fields and harbor quays,
    And birdies asleep in the forks of the trees.

The squalling cat and the squeaking mouse,
    The howling dog by the door of the house,
The bat that lies in bed at noon,
    All love to be out by the light of the moon.

The Owl in the Tree

There was an owl lived in an oak,
    Whiskey, whaskey, wheedle;
The only words he ever spoke
    Were fiddle, faddle, feedle.

An old man chanced to come that way,
    Whiskey, whaskey, wheedle;
Says he, "I see you, silly bird,
    So fiddle, faddle, feedle."

The Wise Old Owl

A wise old owl sat in an oak.

The more he heard, the less he spoke;

The less he spoke, the more he heard.

Why aren't we all like that wise old bird?

Counting Rhymes

One, Two, Buckle My Shoe

One, two, buckle my shoe.

Three, four, knock at the door.

Five, six, pick up sticks.

Seven, eight, lay them straight.

Nine, ten, a good fat hen.

One for the Money

One for the money,

And two for the show,

Three to get ready,

And four to go.

A Counting-Out Rhyme

Hickery, dickery, 6 and 7,
Alabone, Crackabone, 10 and 11,
Spin, spun, muskidun,
Twiddle 'em, twaddle 'em, 21.

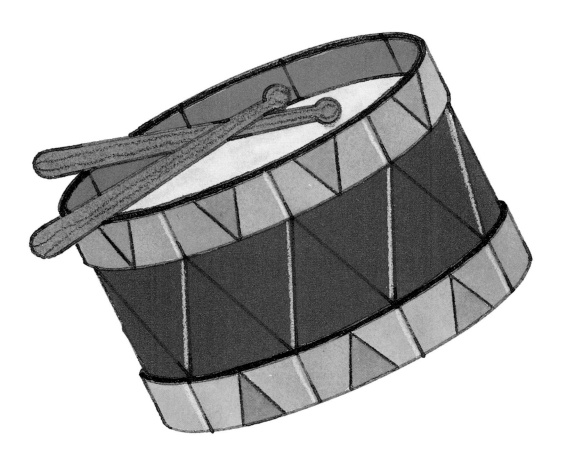

Hot Cross Buns

Hot cross buns! Hot cross buns!
One a penny, two a penny,
Hot cross buns!

If you have no daughters,
Give them to your sons;
One a penny, two a penny,
Hot cross buns!

One, Two, Three

One, two, three, four, five,
    Once I caught a fish alive.
Six, seven, eight, nine, ten,
    But I let it go again.
Why did you let it go?
    Because it bit my finger so.
Which finger did it bite?
    The little one upon the right.

One to Ten

One, two, three, four, five!
Once I caught a hare alive.
Six, seven, eight, nine, ten!
I let her go again.

Three Young Rats

Three young rats with black felt hats,

    Three young ducks with white straw flats,

Three young dogs with curling tails,

    Three young cats with demi-veils,

Went out to walk with two young pigs

    In satin vests and sorrel wigs.

But suddenly it chanced to rain,

    And so they all went home again.

Three Little Kittens

Three little kittens,
  They lost their mittens.
And they began to cry,
  "Oh, mother dear, we sadly fear
That we have lost our mittens."

"Oh dear, don't fear,
  My little kittens.
Come in and have some pie."

Three Times Round

Three times round goes our gallant ship,

And three times round goes she.

Three times round goes our gallant ship,

And sinks to the bottom of the sea.

Finger and Toes

Every lady in this land
    Has twenty nails, upon each hand
Five, and twenty on hands and feet:
    All this is true, without deceit.

Yummy
Rhymes

Pease Porridge Hot

Pease porridge hot,
Pease porridge cold,
Pease porridge in the pot
Nine days old.
Some like it hot,
Some like it cold,
Some like it in the pot,
Nine days old.

Polly, Put the Kettle On

Polly, put the kettle on,
   Polly, put the kettle on,
Polly, put the kettle on,
   We'll all have tea.

Sukey, take it off again,
   Sukey, take it off again,
Sukey, take it off again,
   They've all gone away.

Start the fire and make the toast,
   Put the muffins down to roast,
Start the fire and make the toast,
   We'll all have tea.

Up in the Green Orchard

Up in the green orchard
There is a green tree,
The finest of apples
That you ever did see.
The apples are ripe,
And ready to fall,
And Reuben and Robin
Shall gather them all.

Goober and I

Goober and I were baked in a pie,
And it was wonderful hot.
We had nothing to pay
The baker that day
So we crept out and ran away.

Two Make It

Two make it,
Two bake it,
Two break it.

Little Miss Tucket

Little Miss Tucket
   Sat on a bucket,
Eating some peaches and cream.
   There came a grasshopper
Who tried hard to stop her,
   But she said, "Go away, or I'll scream."

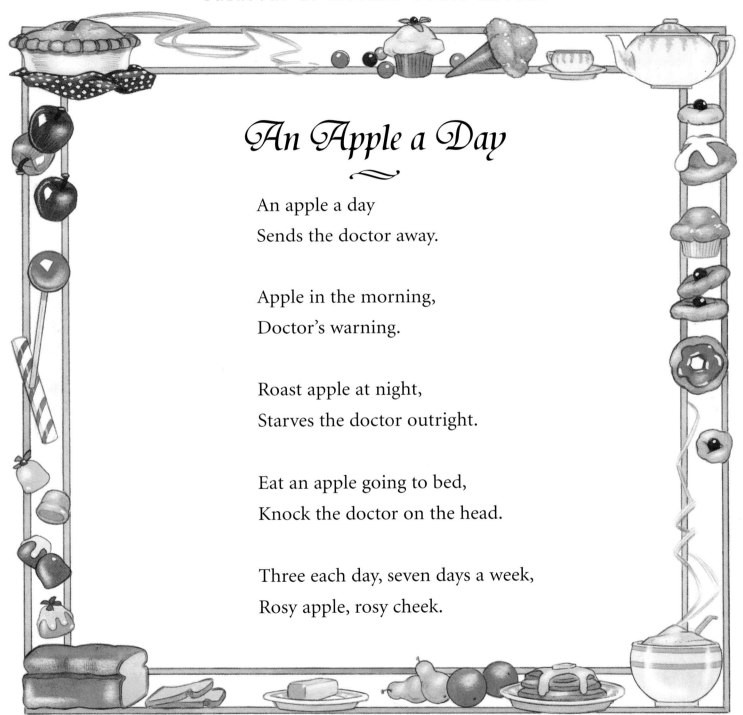

An Apple a Day

An apple a day
Sends the doctor away.

Apple in the morning,
Doctor's warning.

Roast apple at night,
Starves the doctor outright.

Eat an apple going to bed,
Knock the doctor on the head.

Three each day, seven days a week,
Rosy apple, rosy cheek.

When Jack's a Very Good Boy

When Jack's a very good boy,

He shall have cakes and custard;

But when he does nothing but cry,

He shall have nothing but mustard.

Green Cheese

Green cheese, yellow laces,
 Up and down the marketplaces;
Turn, cheeses, turn.

On Christmas Eve

On Christmas Eve I turned the spit;
    I burnt my fingers, I feel it yet;
The sparrow it flew right over the table,
    The pot began to play with the ladle;
The ladle stood up like an angry man,
    And vowed he'd fight the frying pan;
The frying pan hid behind the door
    Said he never saw the like before;
And the kitchen clock I was going to wind,
    Said he never saw the like behind.

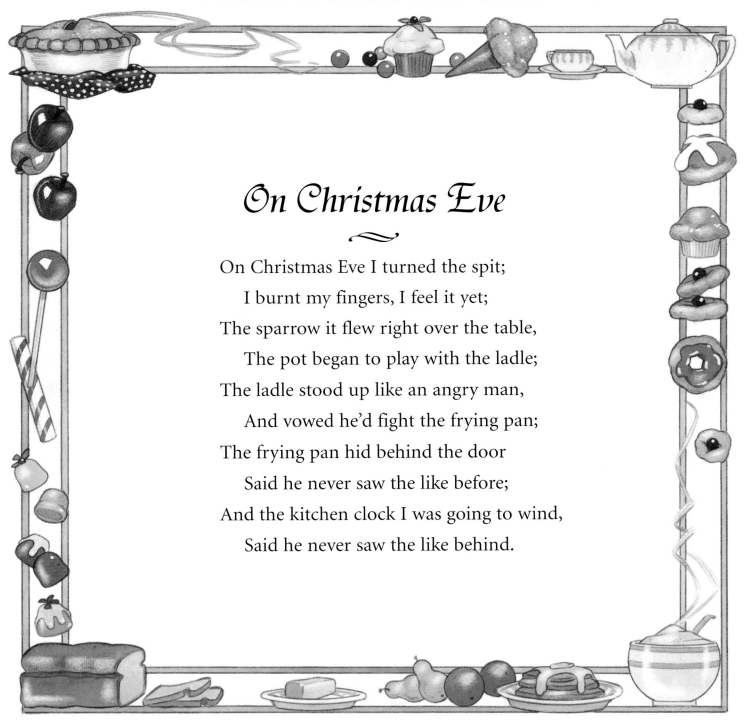

Betty Botter

Betty Botter bought some butter,
  But, she said, the butter's bitter;
If I put it in my batter,
  It will make my batter bitter,
But a bit of better butter
  Will make my batter better.
So she bought a bit of butter,
  Better than her bitter butter,
And she put it in her batter
  And the batter was not bitter.
So it was better Betty Botter bought
  A bit of better butter.

A Big Fat Bowl of Dumplings

A big fat bowl of dumplings,
    Boiling in the pot;
Sugar them and butter them,
    Then eat them while they're hot.

Favorite Rhymes

Sing a Song of Sixpence

Sing a song of sixpence,
A pocket full of rye;
Four-and-twenty blackbirds
Baked in a pie!

When the pie was opened,
The birds began to sing!
Wasn't that a dainty dish
To set before the king?

Peter Pumpkin-Eater

Peter, Peter, pumpkin-eater,

    Had a wife and couldn't keep her.

He put her in a pumpkin shell,

    And there he kept her very well.

Old Mother Hubbard

Old Mother Hubbard
　　Went to the cupboard
To give her poor dog a bone.

When she got there,
　　The cupboard was bare,
And so her poor dog had none.

Old Mother Goose

Old Mother Goose,

When she wanted to wander,

Would ride through the air

On a very fine gander.

There Was an Old Woman

There was an old woman
  Who lived in a shoe.
She had so many children,
  She didn't know what to do.
She gave them some broth
  Without any bread.
She kissed them all sweetly
  And sent them to bed.

Jack Sprat

Jack Sprat could eat no fat.

His wife could eat no lean.

And so between them both, you see,

They licked the platter clean.

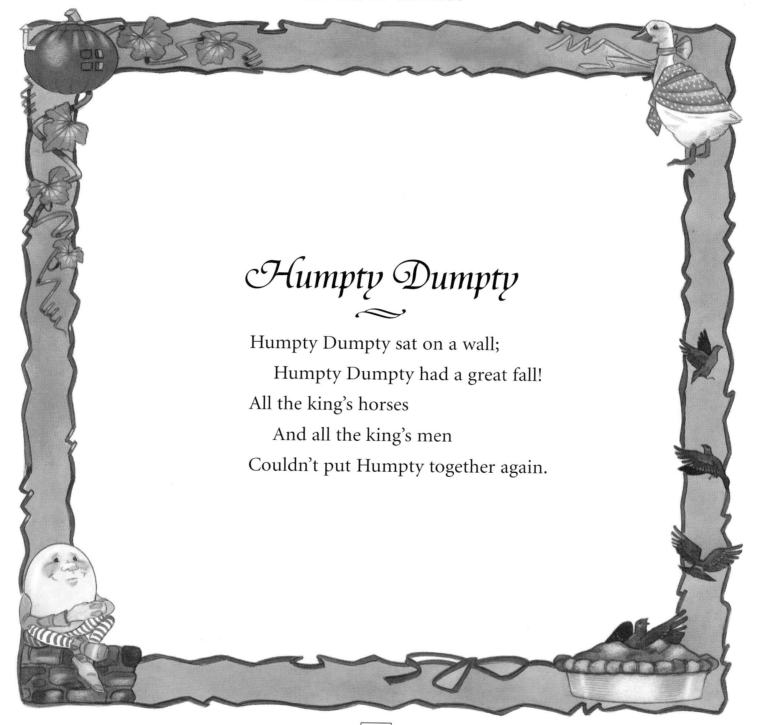

Humpty Dumpty

Humpty Dumpty sat on a wall;
　　Humpty Dumpty had a great fall!
All the king's horses
　　And all the king's men
Couldn't put Humpty together again.

Little Bo-Peep

Little Bo-Peep has lost her sheep,
And can't tell where to find them.
Leave them alone,
And they'll come home,
Wagging their tails behind them.

Old King Cole

Old King Cole
    Was a merry old soul,
And a merry old soul was he;
    He called for his pipe,
And he called for his bowl,
    And he called for his fiddlers three.

Puppy Tales

Where Has My Little Dog Gone

Oh, where, oh, where has my little dog gone?

Oh, where, oh, where can he be?

With his ears cut short and his tail cut long,

Oh, where, oh, where can he be?

Ride Away

Ride away, ride away, Johnny shall ride,

And he shall have kitty cat tied to one side;

And he shall have little dog tied to the other;

And Johnny shall ride to see his grandmother.

What Are Little Boys Made Of

What are little boys made of, made of?

What are little boys made of?

Snips and snails, and puppy-dogs' tails;

That's what little boys are made of, made of.

What are little girls made of, made of?

What are little girls made of?

Sugar and spice, and all things nice,

That's what little girls are made of, made of.

My Dog Spot

I have a white dog
  Whose name is Spot,
And he's sometimes white
  And he's sometimes not.
But whether he's white
  Or whether he's not,
There's a patch on his ear
  That makes him Spot.

He has a tongue
  That is long and pink,
And he lolls it out
  When he wants to think.

Continued on next page

He seems to think most
    When the weather is hot
He's a wise sort of dog,
    Is my dog, Spot.

He likes a bone
    And he likes a ball,
But he doesn't care
    For a cat at all.
He waggles his tail
    And he knows what's what,
So I'm glad that he's my dog,
    My dog, Spot.

Two Little Dogs

Two little dogs sat by the fire,

Next to a pile of coal-dust,

When one dog said to the other dog,

"If you won't talk, why, I must."

Mother Quack's Dog and Cat

Old Mother Quack
  Lived in a shack
Along with her dog and cat;
  What they ate I can't tell
But it's known very well
  That not one of the party was fat.

Old Mother Quack
  Scoured out her shack
And washed both her dog and cat;
  The cat scratched her nose,
And no one quite knows
  Who was the gainer by that?

I'm Just a Little Puppy

I'm just a little puppy and as good as can be,
And why they call me naughty I'm sure I cannot see,
I've only carried off one shoe and torn the baby's hat,
And chased the ducks and spilled the milk—
there's nothing bad in that!

Bow-Wow

Bow-wow, says the dog;

Mew-mew, says the cat;

Grunt, grunt, goes the hog;

And squeak, goes the rat.

Chirp, chirp, says the sparrow;

Caw, caw, says the crow;

Quack, quack, says the duck;

And what cuckoos say, you know.

Continued on next page

So, with sparrows and cuckoos,
  With rats and with dogs,
With ducks and with crows,
  With cats and with hogs,

A fine song I have made,
  To please you, mommy dear;
And if it is well sung,
  'Twill be charming to hear.

Caesar's Song

Bow-wow-wow!
 Whose dog art thou?
Little Tom Tinker's dog,
 Bow-wow-wow!

Leg Over Leg

Leg over leg,

    As the dog went to Dover;

When he came to a fence,

    Jump, he went over.

Hark! Hark!

Hark, hark, the dogs do bark!

Beggars are coming to town;

Some in jags, and some in rags,

And some in velvet gown.

Colorful Rhymes

Little Boy Blue

Little Boy Blue,
Come, blow your horn.
The sheep's in the meadow,
The cow's in the corn.

Where's the little boy
Who looks after the sheep?
He's under the haystack
Fast asleep.

Gray Goose

Gray goose and gander,
Waft your wings together
And carry the king's daughter
Over the one-strand river.

Three Gray Geese

Three gray geese
    In a green field grazing;
Gray were the geese
    And green was the grazing.

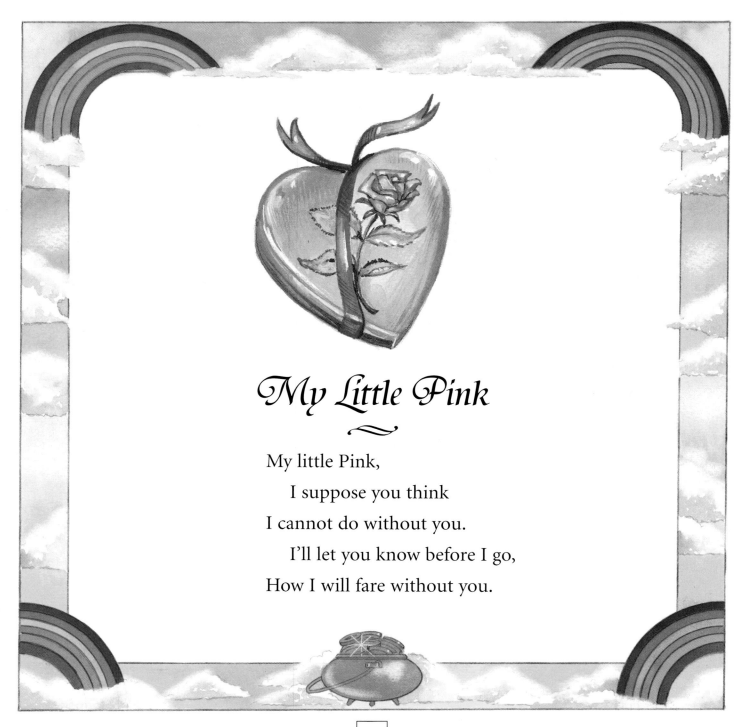

My Little Pink

My little Pink,

    I suppose you think

I cannot do without you.

    I'll let you know before I go,

How I will fare without you.

Roses Are Red

Roses are red,

Violets are blue,

Sugar is sweet,

And so are you!

Dressed in Blue

Those dressed in blue
Have loves true;
In green and white,
Forsaken quite.

Blue Ribbon

If you love me, love me true,

　Send me a ribbon, and let it be blue;

If you do not, let it be seen,

　Send me a ribbon, a ribbon of green.

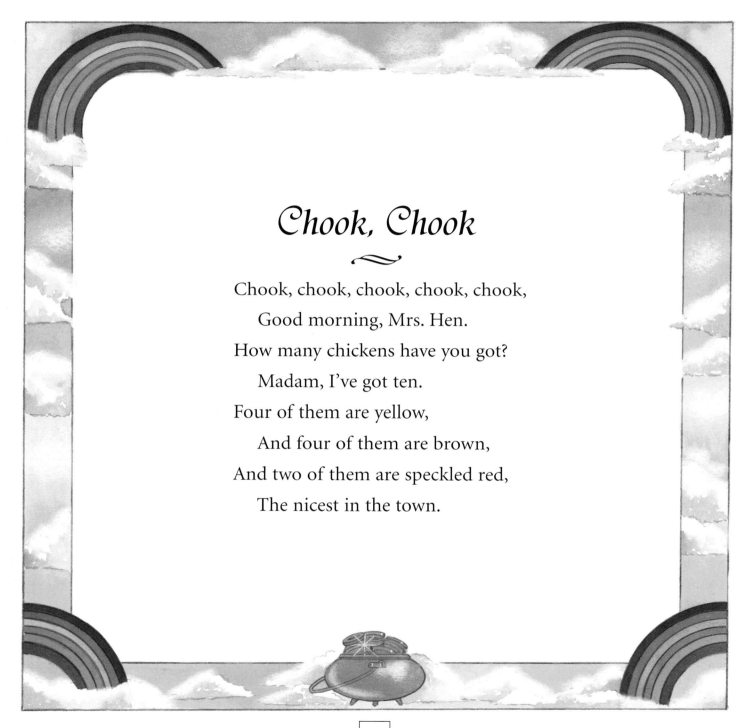

Chook, Chook

Chook, chook, chook, chook, chook,
Good morning, Mrs. Hen.
How many chickens have you got?
Madam, I've got ten.
Four of them are yellow,
And four of them are brown,
And two of them are speckled red,
The nicest in the town.

The Brown Owl

The brown owl sits in the ivy bush,
And she looks wondrous wise,
With a horny beak beneath her cowl,
And a pair of large round eyes.

Little Gray Horse

John Cook had a little gray horse;
  Hee, haw, hum.
When riding he went back and forth;
  Hee, haw, hum.

Little Green House

There was a little green house,
 And in the little green house
There was a little brown house,
 And in the little brown house
There was a little yellow house,
 And in the little yellow house
There was a little white house,
 And in the little white house
There was a little heart.

Jolly Red Nose

Nose, nose, jolly red nose,
And what gave you
That jolly red nose?
Nutmeg and ginger,
Cinnamon and cloves,
That's what gave me
This jolly red nose.

Kitten Yarns

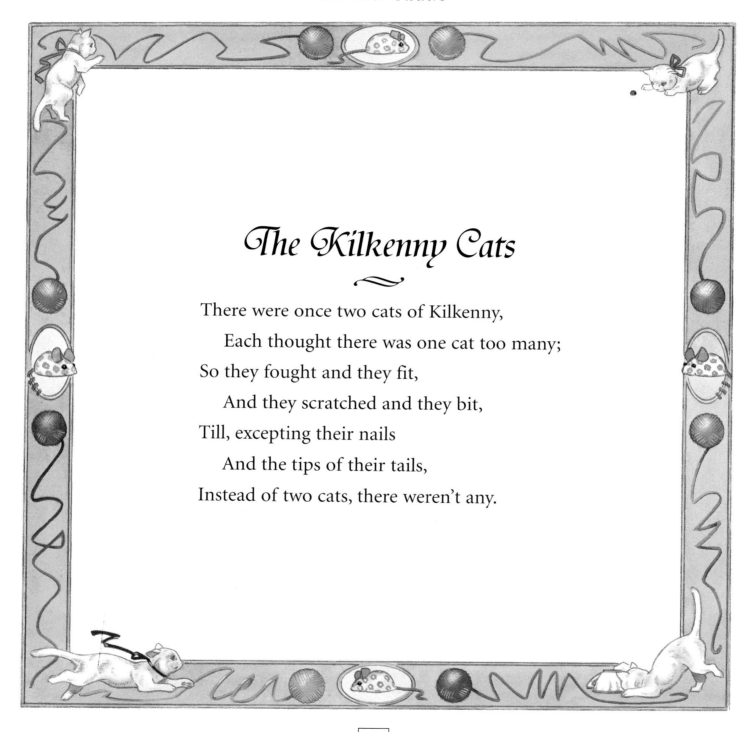

The Kilkenny Cats

There were once two cats of Kilkenny,
    Each thought there was one cat too many;
So they fought and they fit,
    And they scratched and they bit,
Till, excepting their nails
    And the tips of their tails,
Instead of two cats, there weren't any.

Ho My Kitten

Ho my kitten, a kitten,
　　And ho! My kitten, my deary!
Such a sweet pet as this
　　Was neither far nor neary.

Here we go up, up, up,
　　Here we go down, down, down,
Here we go backwards and forwards,
　　And here we go round, round, round.

Little Kitty

I like little kitty,
     Her coat is so warm,
And if I don't tease her
     She'll do me no harm;
So I'll not pull her tail,
     Nor drive her away,
But kitty and I
     Very gently will play.

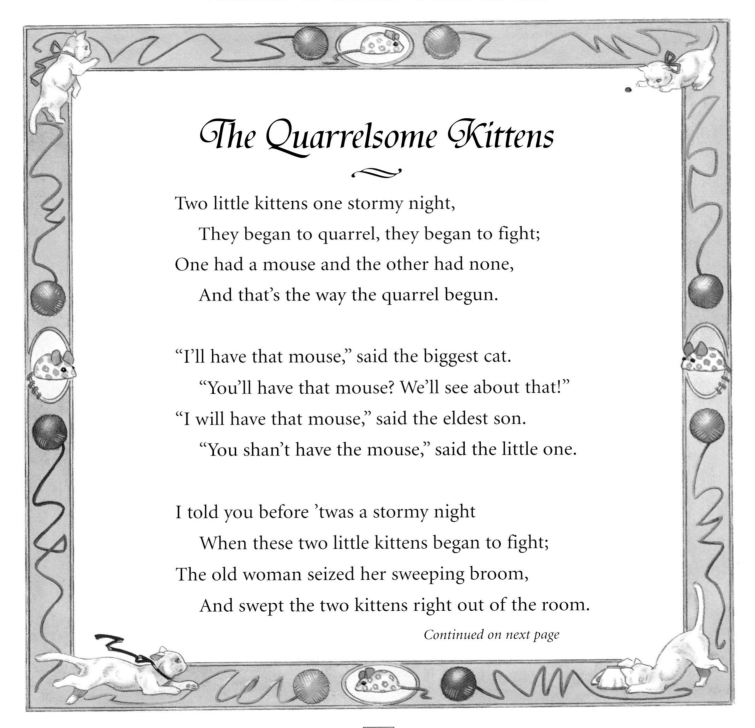

The Quarrelsome Kittens

Two little kittens one stormy night,
　　They began to quarrel, they began to fight;
One had a mouse and the other had none,
　　And that's the way the quarrel begun.

"I'll have that mouse," said the biggest cat.
　　"You'll have that mouse? We'll see about that!"
"I will have that mouse," said the eldest son.
　　"You shan't have the mouse," said the little one.

I told you before 'twas a stormy night
　　When these two little kittens began to fight;
The old woman seized her sweeping broom,
　　And swept the two kittens right out of the room.

Continued on next page

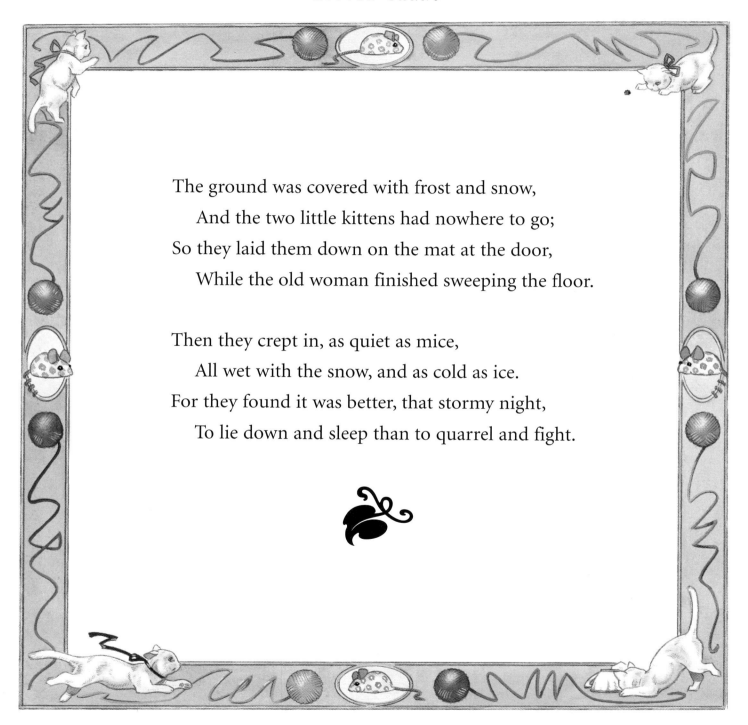

The ground was covered with frost and snow,
　　And the two little kittens had nowhere to go;
So they laid them down on the mat at the door,
　　While the old woman finished sweeping the floor.

Then they crept in, as quiet as mice,
　　All wet with the snow, and as cold as ice.
For they found it was better, that stormy night,
　　To lie down and sleep than to quarrel and fight.

Pussycat, Pussycat

Pussycat, Pussycat where have you been?

I've been to London to visit the Queen.

Pussycat, Pussycat, what did you there?

I frightened a little mouse under her chair.

The Kitten at Play

See the kitten on the wall,
    Sporting with the leaves that fall.
Withered leaves, one, two and three
    Falling from the elder tree,
Through the calm and frosty air
    Of the morning bright and fair.

See the kitten, how she starts,
    Crouches, stretches, paws and darts;
With a tiger-leap halfway
    Now she meets her coming prey.
Lets it go as fast and then
    Has it in her power again.

Continued on next page

Now she works with three or four,
　　Like a graceful juggler;
Quick as he in feats of art,
　　Gracefully she plays her part;
Yet were gazing thousands there,
　　What would little Tabby care?

Kitty Cat and the Dumplings

Kitty cat ate the dumplings, the dumplings,
    Kitty cat ate the dumplings.
Mamma stood by, and cried, "Oh, my!
    Why did you eat the dumplings?"

Mother Cat

There was a mother cat,
Who ate a ball of yarn,
And when she had kittens,
They all had sweaters on.

Sing, Sing

Sing, sing! What shall I sing?

　　The cat's run away with my shoestring.

Do, do, what shall I do?

　　The cat has bit it quite in two.

The Cat and the Fiddle

Hey, diddle, diddle,
  The cat and the fiddle,
The cow jumped
  Over the moon.
The little dog laughed
  To see such sport,
And the dish ran away
  With the spoon.

Two Gray Kits

The two gray kits,
    And the gray kits' mother,
All went over
    The bridge together.

The bridge broke down,
    They all fell in;
"Put on your suits,
    Let's go for a swim."

Ding, Dong, Bell

Ding, dong, bell,
  Kitty's in the well.
Who put her in?
  Little Johnny Green.
Who pulled her out?
  Little Tommy Stout.
What a naughty boy was that
  To try to drown poor kitty cat,
Who never did him any harm,
  And killed the mice in father's barn.

Dame Trot

Dame Trot and her cat
Sat down for to chat;
The Dame sat on this side,
And Kitty on the mat.

"Kitty," says the Dame,
"Can you catch a rat
Or a mouse in the dark?"
"Purr," says the cat.

Big and Little Rhymes

If All the Seas Were One Sea

If all the seas were one sea,

    What a great sea that would be!

And if all the trees were one tree,

    What a great tree that would be!

And if all the axes were one axe,

    What a great axe that would be!

And if all the men were one man,

    What a great man that would be!

And if the great man took the great axe,

    And cut down the great tree,

And let it fall into the great sea,

    What a splish-splash that would be!

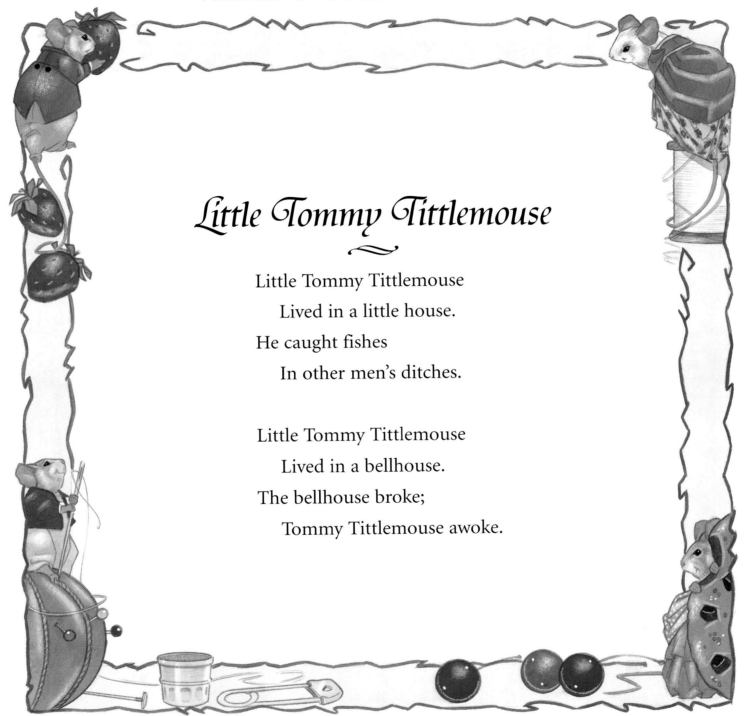

Little Tommy Tittlemouse

Little Tommy Tittlemouse
　　Lived in a little house.
He caught fishes
　　In other men's ditches.

Little Tommy Tittlemouse
　　Lived in a bellhouse.
The bellhouse broke;
　　Tommy Tittlemouse awoke.

Little Girl and Queen

Little girl, little girl,
Where have you been?
Gathering roses
To give to the Queen.
Little girl, little girl,
What gave she you?
She gave me a diamond
As big as my shoe.

The Giant Jim

The giant Jim, great giant grim,

Wears a hat without a brim,

Weighs a ton, and wears a blouse,

And trembles when he meets a mouse.

Jerry Hall

Jerry Hall,

He is so small,

A rat could eat him,

Hat and all.

Little Ships

Little ships

    Must keep the shore;

Larger ships

    May venture more.

Little Nut Tree

I had a little nut tree.
    Nothing would it bear,
But a silver nutmeg
    And a golden pear.
The King of Spain's daughter
    Came to visit me,
And all for the sake
    Of my little nut tree.

Little Tee Wee

Little Tee Wee,
      He went to sea,
In an open boat.
      And while afloat,
The little boat bended,
      And my story's ended.

Twinkle, Twinkle, Little Star

Twinkle, twinkle, little star,

How I wonder what you are,

Up above the world so high,

Like a diamond in the sky.

Twinkle, twinkle, little star,

How I wonder what you are!

Bedtime Rhymes

Wee Willie Winkie

Wee Willie Winkie
    Runs through the town,
Upstairs and downstairs
    In his nightgown,
Rapping at the window,
    Crying through the lock,
"Are the children all in bed?
    Now it's eight o'clock."

Sleep, Baby, Sleep

Sleep, baby, sleep.
> Your father guards the sheep,

Your mother shakes
> The dreamland tree,

And from it fall
> Sweet dreams for thee.

Sleep, baby, sleep.

Hush-a-Bye

Hush-a-bye, baby,
    Lie still with your daddy.
Your mommy has gone to the mill,
    To get some meal to bake a cake.
So please, my dear baby, lie still.

Sleep Tight

Good night,

Sleep tight,

Don't let the bedbugs bite.

Rock-a-Bye, Baby

Rock-a-bye, baby,
On the treetop.
When the wind blows,
The cradle will rock.
When the bough breaks,
The cradle will fall.
Down will come baby,
Cradle and all.

The Cock Crows

The cock crows in the morn
To tell us to rise,
And he that lies late
Will never be wise:
For early to bed
And early to rise
Is the way to be healthy
And wealthy and wise.

Diddle, Diddle, Dumpling

Diddle, diddle, dumpling,
My son John,
Went to bed with his trousers on;
One shoe off, and one shoe on,
Diddle, diddle, dumpling,
My son John.

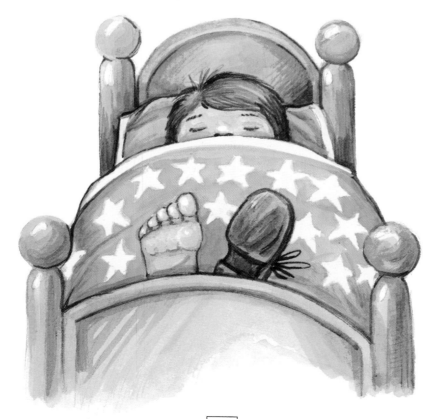

Sleepy Cat

The cat sat asleep
  By the side of the fire.
The mistress snored loud as a pig.

John took up his fiddle,
  By Jenny's desire,
And struck up a bit of a jig.

Come, Let's to Bed

Come, let's to bed,
    Says Sleepy-head.
Sit up awhile, says Slow.

Hang on the pot,
    Says Greedy-gut,
We'll sup before we go.

To bed, to bed,
    Cried Sleepy-head,
But all the rest said no!

It is morning now;
    You must milk the cow,
And tomorrow to bed we go.

Lullaby and Goodnight

~

Lullaby and good night,
> Put your head down and sleep tight,
Lay down now and rest,
> May your slumber be blessed.

Index